Journey of Redemption

George Gentle

Published by George Gentle, 2024.

JOURNEY OF REDEMPTION

First edition. September 15, 2024.

Copyright © 2024 George Gentle.

ISBN: 979-8224879670

Written by George Gentle.

Chapter One: The Crucifixion and the Curse.

The year was 33 AD, and the Roman province of Judea was a land of unrest and turmoil. Marcus, a seasoned Roman centurion, had served the empire for many years, enforcing the will of Rome with unwavering loyalty. His duties often brought him into conflict with the local population, but he carried out his orders with the discipline and efficiency expected of a Roman soldier.

One fateful morning, Marcus received orders from Pontius Pilate, the Roman governor of Judea. A prisoner was to be crucified, a man accused of claiming to be the King of the Jews and inciting rebellion against Rome. The name of the prisoner was Jesus of Nazareth.

Marcus had heard of Jesus, a man who preached love, compassion, and forgiveness. Some called him a prophet, others the Messiah. But to the Roman authorities, he was a threat to their control over the region. Marcus, bound by duty, prepared to carry out the execution.

The day was hot and oppressive as Marcus and his men led Jesus through the streets of Jerusalem. The crowd jeered and spat, their anger and fear palpable. Jesus, though beaten and bloodied, carried himself with a calm and serene dignity that struck Marcus deeply. There was something in his eyes, a profound sadness mixed with an unshakable resolve.

As they reached Golgotha, the place of the skull, Marcus and his men began the grim task of crucifixion. They laid Jesus on the wooden cross, and Marcus, with a heavy heart, drove the nails through his hands and feet. Each strike of the hammer echoed in his soul, a haunting reminder of the suffering he was inflicting.

"Father, forgive them, for they know not what they do," Jesus whispered, his voice filled with compassion even in the face of unimaginable pain.

Marcus paused, his hand trembling. He had carried out many executions, but this one felt different. The words of Jesus pierced his heart, filling him with a sense of guilt and sorrow he had never known.

As the cross was raised and Jesus hung between two thieves, the sky darkened, and a sense of foreboding settled over the land. Marcus stood guard, his mind in turmoil. He watched as Jesus suffered, his body wracked with agony, yet his spirit unbroken.

"Truly, this man was the Son of God," one of the soldiers muttered, echoing the thoughts that had begun to form in Marcus's mind.

As Jesus took his final breath and the earth trembled, Marcus felt a profound sense of loss and regret. He had played a part in the death of an innocent man, a man who had preached love and forgiveness. The weight of his actions bore down on him, and he knew that his life would never be the same.

That night, as Marcus lay in his quarters, he was visited by a figure cloaked in shadow. The figure's eyes burned with an otherworldly light, and its voice was filled with a terrible authority.

"Marcus, for your part in the crucifixion of Jesus of Nazareth, you are cursed to wander the earth for eternity," the figure intoned. "You will seek redemption for your sins, but you will never find peace. You will live forever, bearing the weight of your actions, until the end of time."

Marcus tried to speak, to plead for mercy, but the figure vanished, leaving him alone with his despair. The curse took hold, and Marcus felt a change within him, a sense of timelessness that both terrified and bewildered him.

In the days that followed, Marcus left the Roman army, unable to continue serving an empire that had condemned an innocent man. He began his eternal wanderings, driven by a desire to atone for his part in the crucifixion. He traveled across the ancient world, seeking out those in need, offering his help and protection wherever he could.

Year's passed, and Marcus's journey took him to distant lands, he witnessed the triumphs and tragedies of humanity. His heart remained heavy with the burden of his past, but he found solace in the lives he touched and the good he could do.

He carried the memory of Jesus with him, a reminder of the power of love and forgiveness. Though he knew he could never undo his actions, he was determined to bring light to a world often shrouded in darkness.

And so, Marcus's journey continued, an eternal wanderer bound by a curse but driven by a purpose that transcended time. He sought redemption for his past sins, forever striving to make amends and bring hope to those in need.

Chapter Two: The Arena of Rome.

The year was 64 AD, and the city of Rome was a bustling metropolis, the heart of the mighty Roman Empire. Yet, beneath its grandeur and splendor, there was a darker side—a place where cruelty and spectacle intertwined. The Colosseum, an architectural marvel, was a venue for gladiatorial combat, public executions, and the brutal persecution of Christians.

Marcus, now an eternal wanderer burdened by his curse, had returned to Rome. The city had changed little since he had last served as a centurion, cruelty and injustice remained. He had heard whispers of Christians being rounded up and sentenced to death in the arena, their faith making them targets for the empire's wrath.

One evening, as Marcus walked through the crowded streets, he overheard a group of citizens discussing the upcoming games. A group of Christians was to be fed to the lions, a spectacle meant to entertain the masses and serve as a warning to those who defied Roman authority. The thought of innocent lives being sacrificed for amusement filled Marcus with a deep sense of sorrow and anger.

Determined to intervene, Marcus made his way to the Colosseum. He knew the layout of the arena well, having fought there himself in his younger days. The memories of those brutal contests haunted him, but he pushed them aside, focusing on the task at hand.

As night fell, Marcus slipped into the shadows, making his way to the holding cells where the Christians were being kept. The guards, confident in their control, were lax in their vigilance, allowing Marcus to move undetected. He reached the cell where the prisoners were held and peered through the bars.

Inside, a group of men, women, and children huddled together, their faces etched with fear and resignation. They prayed softly, their faith giving them strength in the face of certain death. Marcus's heart ached for them, and he knew he had to act quickly.

"Quiet," Marcus whispered as he approached the cell door. "I'm here to help you. We need to move quickly."

The prisoners looked up, their eyes wide with surprise and hope. One of the men, a leader of the group, stepped forward. "Who are you?" he asked, his voice trembling.

"A friend," Marcus replied. "There's no time to explain. We must leave now."

Using his lockpicks, Marcus quickly and quietly unlocked the cell door. The prisoners hesitated for a moment, then followed him out into the darkened corridors. Marcus led them through the maze of passageways, avoiding the guards and moving with a sense of urgency.

As they neared the exit, they encountered a group of guards blocking their path. Marcus knew that a confrontation was inevitable. He turned to the prisoners, his expression resolute.

"Stay back," he said. "I'll handle this."

With a swift and practiced motion, Marcus drew his sword and charged the guards. His years as a Roman Centurion made him a formidable opponent, and he fought with a ferocity born of desperation. The guards, taken by surprise, fell one by one, their cries echoing through the corridors.

"Go!" Marcus shouted to the prisoners. "Head for the gate. I'll hold them off."

The Christians, their fear giving way to determination, ran towards the exit. Marcus continued to fight, his movements fluid and precise. He knew that he could not hold off the guards forever, but he was determined to buy the prisoners enough time to escape.

As the last of the Christians disappeared through the gate, Marcus felt a sense of relief. He had saved them, but his own fate was uncertain.

The guards, now fully alerted, began to close in on him. Marcus fought with all his might, but he was eventually overwhelmed and captured.

The next morning, Marcus was brought before the Roman authorities. His actions had not gone unnoticed, and he was sentenced to death for aiding the Christians. As he stood in the arena, awaiting his fate, he felt a sense of peace. He had done what he could to save innocent lives, and that was enough.

But fate had other plans for Marcus, as he stood in the centre of the arena facing a group of ferocious lions, to the astonishment of the crowd the lions did not attack him. Instead, they formed a protective circle around him, their fierce eyes watching the soldiers who attempted to approach. Each time a soldier drew near, the lions would growl and advance, forcing the soldiers to retreat. Marcus, unharmed and calm, stood tall within his living shield, the lions now his unexpected guardians against the threat of the soldiers. His courage moved the crowd, and a wave of sympathy swept through the Colosseum, the Roman authorities sensing the shift in public sentiment decided to spare Marcus's life. As Marcus walked away from the Colosseum, he felt a renewed sense of purpose. His journey was far from over, but he had made a difference. He had saved lives and brought hope to those in need. And so, his eternal wanderings continued, driven by a commitment to helping others and seeking redemption for his past sins.

Chapter Three: The Ashen Sky.

The year was 79 AD, and the city of Pompeii was alive with activity, unaware of the impending doom that loomed over it. Marcus wandered through the bustling streets, the air was filled with the sounds of merchants haggling, children playing, and the distant hum of daily life.

The morning had started like any other, with the sun casting a warm glow over the city. Marcus had been exploring the ancient streets, marveling at the architecture and the vibrant culture. But as the day progressed, an uneasy feeling began to settle in his stomach. The ground beneath his feet trembled slightly, and a low rumble echoed through the air.

He looked up to see a plume of smoke rising from Mount Vesuvius, darkening the sky. Panic began to spread through the streets as people realised what was happening. The volcano was erupting, and there was no time to waste.

Marcus's heart raced as he saw the fear in the eyes of the citizens. He knew he had to help. He quickly made his way to the forum, where a group of women and children had gathered, their faces pale with terror.

"Follow me!" Marcus shouted, trying to keep his voice steady. "We need to get out of the city!"

The group hesitated for a moment, but the urgency in Marcus's voice spurred them into action. They followed him through the narrow streets, dodging falling debris and navigating through the chaos. The air was thick with ash, making it difficult to breathe, and the ground shook violently beneath their feet.

As they made their way towards the city gates, Marcus spotted an elderly woman struggling to keep up. He rushed to her side, supporting her with one arm while urging the others to keep moving.

"Don't stop!" he called out. "We have to keep going!"

The group pressed on, their fear driving them forward. They reached the city gates just as the sky turned an ominous shade of black. The ground shook with such force that it felt as though the earth itself was splitting apart.

Marcus led the group out of the city and into the countryside, where they found temporary shelter in a small grove of trees. They huddled together, watching in horror as Pompeii was consumed by the eruption. The once vibrant city was now a scene of devastation, buried under a blanket of ash and pumice.

For hours, they waited, the sounds of the eruption echoing in their ears. Marcus did his best to comfort the frightened children, telling them stories of heroes and adventures to keep their minds off the disaster unfolding before them.

As the ash began to settle, Marcus knew they couldn't stay in the grove forever. They needed to find a more secure place to wait out the aftermath of the eruption. He stood up, his body aching from the strain of the day's events, and addressed the group.

"We need to keep moving," he said. "There are other towns nearby where we can find help. Stay close and stay together."

With Marcus leading the way, the group set off once more, their spirits buoyed by the knowledge that they had survived the worst of the disaster. They walked for hours, through fields and forests, until they finally reached a small village where they were welcomed with open arms.

The villagers provided food, water, and shelter, and Marcus finally allowed himself to relax. He had done it. He had helped these people escape the destruction of Pompeii. As he sat by the fire that night, listening to the sounds of the village, he couldn't help but feel a sense of gratitude. He had been given a chance to make a difference, and he had seized it.

The memory of that day would stay with him forever, a reminder of the strength and resilience of the human spirit in the face of unimaginable disaster.

Chapter Four: The Fall of Elagabalus.

The year was 222 AD, and the Roman Empire was in a state of turmoil. Emperor Elagabalus, a young and controversial ruler, had ascended to the throne four years earlier. His reign was marked by excess, debauchery, and a blatant disregard for Roman traditions. The emperor's eccentric behavior and shocking antics had alienated the Senate, the military, and the people of Rome.

Marcus, now an eternal wanderer burdened by his curse, had returned to Rome once more. He had witnessed many emperors rise and fall, but Elagabalus's reign was particularly chaotic. Despite the emperor's flaws, Marcus felt a sense of duty to protect the young ruler, hoping to guide him towards a more stable and just rule.

One evening, Marcus found himself at one of Elagabalus's infamous banquets. The opulence and extravagance were overwhelming—golden dishes, rare foods, and elaborate entertainment filled the grand hall. The guests, a mix of nobles and sycophants, indulged in the excess, their laughter and revelry masking the underlying tension.

As Marcus observed the scene, he couldn't help but feel a sense of unease. Elagabalus, dressed in lavish robes and adorned with jewels, presided over the feast with a manic energy. His eyes gleamed with a wild intensity as he humiliated his guests, serving them wax and stone food instead of real meals. The emperor's behavior was erratic and unpredictable, a reflection of the chaos that had come to define his reign.

Marcus approached the emperor, hoping to offer some counsel. "Your Majesty," he said, bowing respectfully, "may I have a word with you?"

Elagabalus looked at Marcus, his expression a mix of curiosity and disdain. "What is it, stranger?" he asked, his voice dripping with sarcasm. "Are you here to lecture me on propriety?"

"Not at all, Your Majesty," Marcus replied calmly. "I am here to offer my assistance. The empire is in turmoil, and your enemies grow bolder by the day. I believe that with the right guidance, you can restore stability and earn the respect of your people."

Elagabalus laughed, a harsh and mocking sound. "You think you can save me, stranger? You think you can change the course of my destiny?"

"I believe that everyone has the potential for redemption," Marcus said, his voice steady. "But it requires a willingness to change, to listen, and to act with wisdom and compassion."

The emperor's laughter faded, replaced by a flicker of uncertainty. For a moment, Marcus thought he had reached him. But then Elagabalus's expression hardened, and he waved dismissively. "Leave me, stranger. I have no need for your advice."

Marcus bowed and stepped back, his heart heavy with disappointment. He had tried to reach the young emperor, but Elagabalus was too consumed by his own excesses and delusions to listen.

As the night wore on, the revelry continued, but the tension in the air grew thicker. Marcus sensed that something was amiss, and his instincts proved correct. A group of Praetorian Guards, led by the emperor's own grandmother, Julia Maesa, had conspired to remove Elagabalus from power. They had grown tired of his erratic behavior and feared for the future of the empire.

In the early hours of the morning, the guards stormed the palace, their swords drawn. Chaos erupted as they cut down anyone who stood in their way. Marcus fought valiantly, trying to protect the emperor, but the odds were overwhelming.

"Elagabalus!" Marcus shouted, his voice rising above the din. "We must leave now!"

The emperor, now fully aware of the danger, looked at Marcus with a mixture of fear and desperation. "Help me, stranger!" he cried, his earlier arrogance replaced by a plea for salvation.

Marcus grabbed Elagabalus's arm and led him through the palace, fighting off the guards as they went. But their escape was short-lived. The conspirators had anticipated their move and had blocked all exits.

Surrounded and outnumbered, Marcus and Elagabalus were cornered in a small chamber. The guards closed in, their faces grim and determined. Marcus fought with all his might, but he was eventually overpowered and disarmed.

"Your reign is over, Elagabalus," one of the guards said coldly. "The empire will not suffer your madness any longer."

With a final, desperate look at Marcus, Elagabalus was dragged away. The young emperor's cries echoed through the halls as he was taken to his execution. Marcus, bound and helpless, could only watch as the man he had tried to save was led to his death.

The next day, news of Elagabalus's assassination spread throughout Rome. The emperor's short and notorious reign had come to a violent end, and the city was left to pick up the pieces. Marcus, released from his bonds, wandered the streets, his heart heavy with sorrow and regret.

He had failed to save Elagabalus, but he knew that his journey was far from over. The curse that bound him to eternal wandering also drove him to seek redemption, to help those in need, and to bring light to a world often shrouded in darkness.

And so, Marcus continued his eternal quest, he carried the memory of Elagabalus with him, a reminder of the fragility of power and the importance of compassion and wisdom. His journey was one of endless striving, forever seeking to make amends for his past sins and to bring hope to those who needed it most.

Chapter Five: The Monks of Iona.

The year was 806 AD, and the island of Iona, off the western coast of Scotland, was a place of serene beauty and spiritual devotion. The monks of Iona had dedicated their lives to prayer, study, and the creation of illuminated manuscripts. Among their most treasured works was a gospel-book, a masterpiece of art and faith.

Marcus, the eternal wanderer, had found solace among the monks, drawn to their peaceful way of life and their commitment to preserving knowledge and faith. He had spent several months on the island, helping with daily tasks and learning from the monks' wisdom. But the tranquility of Iona was about to be shattered.

One fateful morning, as the monks went about their prayers and duties, the sound of distant horns echoed across the island. Marcus, his instincts honed by centuries of experience, recognised the sound immediately. Vikings were approaching, their longships cutting through the waves with deadly intent.

"Brothers, we must prepare," Marcus said urgently, rushing into the abbey. "Vikings are coming. We need to protect the sacred texts and ensure your safety."

The abbot, a wise and venerable man named Brother Ciaran, looked at Marcus with a mixture of fear and determination. "We have little time," he said. "The gospel-book must be saved. It is our most precious work."

Marcus nodded. "Gather what you can carry. We must flee to the mainland. I will do my best to hold them off."

The monks moved quickly, their fear tempered by their faith. They gathered the gospel-book and other valuable manuscripts, wrapping them carefully in cloth. Marcus led them to a hidden path that wound through the hills, offering a chance to escape the impending raid.

As the monks made their way to the path, Marcus turned back to face the approaching longships. The Vikings, fierce and relentless, would show no mercy. He knew that he could not stop them entirely, but he could buy the monks enough time to escape.

With a deep breath, Marcus positioned himself at the entrance to the abbey, his sword drawn. The first of the Viking raiders landed on the shore, their eyes gleaming with the promise of plunder. They charged towards the abbey, their weapons raised.

Marcus fought with a ferocity born of desperation. His centuries of experience made him a formidable opponent, and he cut down the first wave of attackers with swift and precise strikes. But the Vikings were many, and they pressed forward with relentless determination.

"Go!" Marcus shouted to the monks, who were now making their way up the hidden path. "I will hold them off as long as I can."

Brother Ciaran looked back, his eyes filled with gratitude and sorrow. "May God protect you, Marcus," he said. "We will never forget your sacrifice."

As the monks disappeared into the hills, Marcus continued to fight, his movements fluid and deadly. He knew that he could not hold off the Vikings forever, but he was determined to give the monks every possible chance to escape.

The battle raged on, and Marcus felt the weight of his curse bearing down on him. He had seen so much suffering and death over the centuries, but he had also found moments of redemption and hope. This was one of those moments—a chance to protect the innocent and preserve something of great value.

Eventually, the sheer number of Vikings overwhelmed Marcus. He was struck gravely wounded, his fate uncertain. The raiders ransacked the abbey, but the most precious treasures—the gospel-book and the monks—had escaped their grasp.

As Marcus lay wounded on the ground, he watched the longships sail away, their holds filled with plunder. He felt a sense of relief, knowing that the monks had escaped and that the gospel-book was safe. His sacrifice had not been in vain.

In the days that followed, Marcus, weary and wounded, made his way to the mainland, driven by a sense of duty and a desire to ensure the monks' safety.

He eventually found the monks in Kells, a small town in County Meath, Ireland. They had taken refuge in the local monastery, and the gospel-book was safe. The monks welcomed Marcus with open arms, their gratitude evident in their eyes.

"Marcus, you have saved us and our most precious work," Brother Ciaran said, his voice filled with emotion. "We owe you a debt that can never be repaid."

Marcus shook his head, his heart heavy with the weight of his eternal journey. "There is no need for repayment," he said softly. "I am simply glad that you are safe and that the gospel-book is preserved."

The monks continued their work in Kells, and the gospel-book became known as the Book of Kells, a masterpiece of art and faith that would inspire generations to come. Marcus, ever the wanderer, continued his journey, driven by a commitment to helping those in need and seeking redemption for his past sins.

And so, his eternal wanderings continued, guided by a purpose that transcended time.

Chapter Six: The Siege of Jerusalem.

The year was 1099, and the First Crusade had reached its climax. Marcus, ever the wanderer, found himself in the ranks of the French forces under the command of Louis Thierry of Alsace. The crusaders had journeyed far, driven by a fervent desire to reclaim the Holy City of Jerusalem from Muslim control. The air was thick with tension and anticipation as the army prepared to lay siege to the ancient city.

The walls of Jerusalem loomed before them, a formidable barrier that had withstood countless assaults over the centuries. The crusaders, fueled by religious zeal and the promise of glory, were determined to breach the city's defenses. Marcus, though weary of the endless cycle of violence, had joined the crusade in the hope of finding some measure of redemption.

As the siege began, the French forces launched a relentless assault on the city's walls. Siege engines hurled stones and flaming projectiles, while ladders and battering rams were brought to bear against the gates. The defenders fought valiantly, but the sheer force of the crusader army was overwhelming.

Marcus fought alongside his comrades, his skill and experience making him a formidable warrior. Yet, even as he battled, he could not ignore the pangs of guilt that gnawed at his conscience. The indiscriminate slaughter of civilians, the cries of the innocent—these were the horrors of war that he had witnessed countless times before.

As the crusaders breached the walls and poured into the city, chaos erupted. The streets of Jerusalem became a battleground, with soldiers clashing and civilians caught in the crossfire. Marcus moved through the carnage, his heart heavy with sorrow.

In the midst of the chaos, Marcus spotted a young Muslim woman, her eyes wide with terror as she tried to shield her child from the violence. Without hesitation, Marcus rushed to her side, his sword raised to fend off any attackers.

"Stay close to me," he said urgently, his voice steady despite the turmoil around them. "I'll get you to safety."

The woman nodded, her fear giving way to a glimmer of hope. Marcus led her and her child through the war-torn streets, trying to navigate a path to safety. They found refuge in a small, hidden courtyard, where the sounds of battle were muffled by the thick stone walls.

"Thank you," the woman said, her voice trembling with emotion. "You saved our lives."

Marcus offered a faint smile, his heart aching with the weight of his past. "It's the least I can do. My name is Marcus."

"I am Amina," she replied, her eyes filled with gratitude. "And this is my son, Tariq."

In the days that followed, Marcus continued to protect Amina and Tariq, ensuring their safety amidst the chaos of the siege. As they spent time together, a bond began to form between them, born of shared hardship and mutual respect.

When the fighting finally subsided and the crusaders claimed victory, Marcus made a decision that would change his life forever. He asked Amina to marry him, and she accepted, her heart touched by his kindness and bravery.

Their marriage was a source of joy and solace for Marcus, a rare moment of happiness in his long and tumultuous life. Amina's love and compassion brought light to his darkness, and for a time, he allowed himself to believe that he had found a measure of peace.

Years passed, and Marcus and Amina built a life together. He raised Tariq as his own, and their home became a sanctuary of love and warmth. Yet, as the years went by, the reality of Marcus's immortality became increasingly apparent. While he remained unchanged, Amina grew older, her once-vibrant spirit gradually dimming with the passage of time.

Marcus watched with a heavy heart as the woman he loved aged before his eyes. He cared for her with unwavering devotion, but he could not escape the knowledge that their time together was finite. The inevitability of her mortality was a cruel reminder of the curse that bound him.

One quiet evening, as the sun set over the horizon, Amina lay in their bed, her breathing shallow and laboured. Marcus sat by her side, holding her hand, his heart breaking with each passing moment.

"Marcus," Amina whispered, her voice weak but filled with love, "you have given me a life I never dreamed possible. I am grateful for every moment we shared."

Tears filled Marcus's eyes as he leaned down to kiss her forehead. "And I am grateful for you, Amina. You brought light to my darkness. I will love you always."

With a final, gentle sigh, Amina closed her eyes and slipped away, leaving Marcus alone once more. The pain of her loss was a wound that would never fully heal, a reminder of the fleeting nature of mortal life.

As the years turned into centuries, Marcus continued his eternal wanderings, carrying the memory of Amina with him. Her love and the time they shared became a source of strength, a beacon of hope in a world often shrouded in darkness.

Though his journey was far from over, Marcus knew that he had been blessed with a rare and precious gift—the love of a woman who had seen beyond his curse and embraced him for who he was. And in that love, he found a measure of redemption, a reminder that even in the face of eternity, the bonds of the heart could transcend time.

Chapter Seven: The Siege of Calais.

The year was 1347, and the Hundred Years' War between England and France was in full swing. The town of Calais, a strategic port on the northern coast of France, had been under siege by the English forces for nearly a year. The townspeople were starving, their supplies exhausted, and their hope dwindling. The situation was dire, and the prospect of surrender loomed large.

Marcus, ever the wanderer, found himself in the besieged town, drawn by the suffering and the need for aid. He had seen many sieges in his long life, but the desperation of Calais was palpable. The English forces, led by King Edward III, were determined to capture the town, and their blockade had left the inhabitants with no means of escape or resupply.

As the days turned into weeks, the situation grew increasingly grim. The town's leaders, knowing that they could not hold out much longer, decided to negotiate a surrender. King Edward, however, demanded a harsh price for sparing the town: six of its leading citizens, the burghers, were to present themselves before him, barefoot and with nooses around their necks, ready to be executed.

The news of the king's demand spread quickly through the town, and the people were filled with despair. The burghers, knowing that their sacrifice could save the lives of their fellow citizens, bravely stepped forward. Among them was Eustache de Saint Pierre, a wealthy and respected merchant who had long been a pillar of the community.

Marcus, moved by the courage and selflessness of the burghers, resolved to do everything in his power to help them. He knew that their sacrifice could not be in vain, and he was determined to find a way to save their lives.

On the appointed day, the six burghers, dressed in simple tunics and barefoot, made their way to the gates of Calais. The townspeople lined the streets, their faces etched with sorrow and fear. Marcus walked alongside the burghers, his heart heavy with the weight of their impending fate.

As they reached the English camp, the burghers were brought before King Edward. The king, a stern and imposing figure, looked down upon them with a mixture of disdain and satisfaction. The nooses were placed around their necks, and the burghers stood ready to meet their fate.

But Marcus was not willing to let them die. He had learned over the centuries that even in the darkest moments, there was always a glimmer of hope. He approached the king, his demeanor calm and respectful.

"Your Majesty," Marcus said, bowing deeply, "I implore you to show mercy to these brave men. Their sacrifice is a testament to their love for their town and their people. Spare their lives, and you will be remembered not only as a great conqueror but also as a just and compassionate ruler."

King Edward's eyes narrowed as he regarded Marcus. "And who are you to make such a plea?" he demanded.

"I am but a humble servant of humanity," Marcus replied, his voice steady. "I have seen much suffering in my life, and I know that mercy can be a powerful force for good. These men have shown great courage. Let their lives be a symbol of your magnanimity."

The king's advisors murmured among themselves, some urging him to show clemency, while others argued for the execution. Queen Philippa, Edward's wife, who had been watching the proceedings with a heavy heart, stepped forward.

"My lord," she said softly, placing a hand on the king's arm, "I beg you to spare these men. Their bravery and selflessness have touched my heart. Show them mercy, and it will be a testament to your greatness."

King Edward looked into his wife's eyes, seeing the sincerity and compassion there. After a long moment, he nodded. "Very well," he said, his voice carrying the weight of his decision. "I will spare their lives."

A collective sigh of relief swept through the crowd as the nooses were removed from the burghers' necks. Tears of gratitude and joy filled their eyes as they realised that their lives had been spared. Marcus felt a profound sense of fulfillment, knowing that he had played a part in saving these brave men.

The burghers were escorted back to Calais, where they were greeted as heroes. The townspeople, who had feared the worst, now celebrated their deliverance. Marcus watched from the sidelines, his heart filled with a mixture of joy and sorrow. He knew that the road ahead would still be difficult, but for now, there was hope.

As the days passed, Marcus continued to aid the people of Calais, helping to rebuild and restore their town. The memory of the six burghers and their courage remained a beacon of hope and resilience, a reminder that even in the darkest times, there was always the possibility of redemption.

And so, Marcus's eternal wanderings continued, driven by a commitment to helping those in need and seeking redemption for his past sins.

Chapter Eight: The Plague of Shadows.

The year was 1350, and Europe was in the grip of one of the most devastating pandemics in human history—the Bubonic Plague. The Black Death, as it came to be known, swept across the continent with a ferocity that left entire towns and cities decimated. The air was thick with the stench of death, and the streets were filled with the cries of the dying and the wails of the bereaved.

Marcus, ever the wanderer, found himself traveling through this landscape of despair. His centuries of experience had taught him much about medicine and healing, and he was determined to use his knowledge to help those in need. The plague was a relentless and merciless foe, but Marcus's resolve was unyielding.

As he journeyed from village to village, Marcus encountered scenes of unimaginable suffering. The plague spared no one—rich or poor, young or old. The infected were marked by painful swellings, high fever, and a rapid decline that often ended in death within days. Fear and panic gripped the populace, and many turned to superstition and scapegoating in their desperation.

In one small village, Marcus found a makeshift infirmary set up in a church. The pews had been pushed aside to make room for the sick, who lay on straw mats, their faces contorted in pain. The local priest, Father Thomas, was doing his best to provide comfort and care, but the sheer number of afflicted was overwhelming.

"Father Thomas," Marcus said, approaching the weary priest, "I have some knowledge of medicine. Let me help."

The priest looked up, his eyes filled with exhaustion and gratitude. "Bless you, my son. We need all the help we can get."

Marcus set to work, moving among the sick with a calm and steady demeanor. He cleaned wounds, administered herbal remedies, and offered words of comfort to those in their final moments. His presence brought a measure of hope to the beleaguered villagers, and his tireless efforts did not go unnoticed.

One evening, as Marcus tended to a young girl burning with fever, Father Thomas approached him. "You have a gift, Marcus," the priest said softly. "Your compassion and skill are a blessing to us all."

Marcus shook his head, his expression somber. "I do what I can, but it never feels like enough. The plague is relentless, and so many are beyond saving."

Father Thomas placed a hand on Marcus's shoulder. "Even in the face of such darkness, your efforts bring light. You give people hope, and that is a powerful thing."

As the days turned into weeks, Marcus continued his journey across Europe, moving from one stricken community to the next. He encountered scenes of horror and heartbreak, but also moments of incredible resilience and humanity. In one town, he met a group of nuns who had dedicated themselves to caring for the sick, their faith and compassion shining brightly amidst the gloom.

In another village, Marcus found a family hiding in their home, terrified of the outside world. He spent hours with them, offering reassurance and practical advice on how to avoid infection. His presence brought them a sense of peace, and they began to emerge from their isolation, determined to help their neighbors.

Despite his best efforts, Marcus knew that he could not save everyone. The plague was a force of nature, indifferent to the suffering it caused. Yet, he refused to give in to despair. Each life he touched, each person he comforted, was a victory against the darkness.

One night, as Marcus rested by a campfire on the outskirts of a plague-ravaged town, he reflected on his journey. The memories of those he had helped and those he had lost weighed heavily on his heart. The faces of the dying haunted his dreams, but so too did the moments of kindness and courage he had witnessed.

As he stared into the flickering flames, Marcus made a silent vow. He would continue to fight against the darkness, to bring hope and healing wherever he could. His journey was far from over, and the road ahead would be filled with challenges, but he was determined to make a difference.

The next morning, Marcus rose with the dawn and continued his travels. The plague had not yet run its course, and there were still countless lives in need of aid. He moved with purpose, his heart heavy with the weight of his past but buoyed by the knowledge that his actions, however small, could bring light to a world shrouded in shadow.

And so, Marcus's eternal wanderings continued, driven by a commitment to helping those in need and seeking redemption for his past sins. He was forever striving to bring light to a world often shrouded in darkness.

Chapter Nine: The Martyrdom of Joan of Arc.

The year was 1431, and the Hundred Years' War between England and France was nearing its end. The conflict had seen many heroes and tragedies, but none as compelling as the story of Joan of Arc. A young peasant girl who claimed to have been guided by divine visions, Joan had risen to prominence as a leader of the French forces, inspiring her countrymen with her courage and faith.

Marcus, ever the wanderer, had heard of Joan's exploits and felt a deep admiration for her. Her unwavering conviction and selfless dedication to her cause resonated with him, stirring memories of his own struggles for redemption. When he learned that Joan had been captured by the English and was to be tried for heresy, Marcus knew he had to act.

He traveled to Rouen, where Joan was being held in a grim and foreboding castle. The trial was a farce, a mockery of justice orchestrated by those who sought to discredit and destroy her. Despite her eloquent defense and steadfast faith, the outcome was never in doubt. Joan was condemned to death by burning at the stake.

Marcus's heart ached with the injustice of it all. He had seen many innocent lives lost over the centuries, but Joan's fate felt particularly cruel. She was a beacon of hope and inspiration, and her death would be a profound loss for France and for all who believed in her cause.

Determined to save her, Marcus devised a plan. He knew the castle's layout and the routines of the guards, and he believed that with careful timing and a bit of luck, he could rescue Joan from her cell and spirit her away to safety. The night before her execution, he made his move.

Under the cover of darkness, Marcus slipped into the castle, his movements silent and deliberate. He navigated the labyrinthine corridors, avoiding the guards and making his way to the dungeon where Joan was being held. As he approached her cell, he could hear her praying softly, her voice filled with a serene and unshakable faith.

"Joan," Marcus whispered urgently as he reached the barred door. "I'm here to help you. We must leave now."

Joan looked up, her eyes wide with surprise and hope. "Who are you?" she asked, her voice trembling.

"A friend," Marcus replied. "There's no time to explain. We must go before the guards return."

Joan hesitated for a moment, then nodded. "Very well. I trust you."

Marcus worked quickly to unlock the cell door, his hands steady despite the urgency of the situation. Just as he was about to free Joan, the sound of approaching footsteps echoed through the corridor. The guards were returning.

"Hide," Marcus whispered, his heart pounding. "I'll distract them."

Joan retreated into the shadows of her cell as Marcus stepped into the corridor, his mind racing. He needed to buy time, to find a way to lead the guards away from Joan's cell. But as the guards rounded the corner, their eyes fell upon him, and they raised the alarm.

"Intruder!" one of the guards shouted, drawing his sword.

Marcus fought with all his might, his centuries of experience making him a formidable opponent. But the odds were against him, and more guards quickly arrived, overwhelming him. He was captured and dragged before the castle's commander, who ordered him to be thrown into a cell of his own.

As dawn broke, Marcus could hear the preparations for Joan's execution. The sound of hammering as the stake was erected, the murmurs of the gathered crowd, and the prayers of the priests. His heart ached with helplessness and sorrow. He had failed to save her.

From his cell, Marcus could see the courtyard where Joan was to be executed. She was led out, her hands bound, her face serene and resolute. The crowd watched in silence as she was tied to the stake, the kindling piled around her feet.

As the flames were lit, Marcus felt a profound sense of despair. He could only watch helplessly as the fire grew, engulfing Joan in its merciless embrace. Her voice, clear and unwavering, rose above the crackling flames as she called out to God, her faith unbroken even in the face of death.

"Jesus, Jesus, Jesus," she cried, her words a testament to her unshakable belief.

Tears streamed down Marcus's face as he watched the flames consume her. Joan's death was a tragedy, a senseless act of cruelty that left a deep scar on his soul. He had seen many horrors in his long life, but this was one of the hardest to bear.

As the fire burned out and the crowd dispersed, Marcus was left alone with his grief. He had failed to save Joan, but her spirit and her courage would live on in his heart. She had been a beacon of hope and inspiration, and her martyrdom would only strengthen the resolve of those who believed in her cause.

In the years that followed, Marcus was eventually released from his cell and left Rouen, his heart heavy with sorrow. He continued his eternal wanderings, driven by a commitment to helping those in need and seeking redemption for his past sins. The memory of Joan's bravery and faith remained with him, a reminder that even in the darkest times, there was always the possibility of light.

And so, Marcus's journey continued, an eternal wanderer bound by a curse but driven by a purpose that transcended time.

Chapter Ten: The Enigmatic Smile.

Marcus found himself walking the cobblestone streets of Florence in the late 15th century. The city was alive with the sounds of artisans at work, the chatter of merchants, and the vibrant energy of a society on the cusp of greatness.

One afternoon, as he wandered through the bustling marketplace, he found himself drawn to a small workshop tucked away in a quiet alley. The sign above the door read "Leonardo da Vinci, Artist and Inventor." Intrigued, Marcus stepped inside, the scent of oil paints and wood shavings filling the air.

The workshop was a hive of activity, with apprentices bustling about, mixing pigments and preparing canvases. At the centre of it all stood Leonardo da Vinci himself, a man of striking presence with keen, intelligent eyes and a beard that framed his face like a lion's mane. He was deeply engrossed in a sketch, his hand moving with fluid precision.

"Excuse me, Maestro," Marcus said, his voice tinged with awe. "I didn't mean to intrude."

Leonardo looked up, a curious smile playing on his lips. "No intrusion at all, my friend. What brings you to my humble workshop?"

"I've always admired your work," Marcus replied. "Your inventions, your paintings—they're extraordinary."

Leonardo's eyes sparkled with amusement. "Flattery will get you everywhere. Come, let me show you what I'm working on."

Marcus followed Leonardo to a large easel, where a canvas was propped up. The sketch on it was rough, but the outline of a woman's face was already taking shape. Her expression was serene, yet there was a hint of mystery in her eyes.

"I'm trying to capture something elusive," Leonardo explained. "A smile that is both inviting and enigmatic. But it's proving to be quite the challenge."

As Marcus studied the sketch, he felt a strange connection to the image. There was something familiar about the woman's face, something that tugged at the edges of his memory. He turned to Leonardo, a question forming on his lips.

"Have you ever considered using a live model?" Marcus asked. "Someone who embodies the qualities you're trying to capture?"

Leonardo nodded thoughtfully. "Indeed, I have. But finding the right person is no easy task."

Just then, the door to the workshop opened, and a young woman entered. She was dressed simply, but there was an elegance to her movements, a grace that caught Marcus's attention. Her name was Lisa Gherardini, and she had come to commission a portrait for her husband.

Leonardo greeted her warmly, and as they spoke, Marcus couldn't help but notice the way Lisa's eyes sparkled with intelligence and warmth. There was a quiet strength in her demeanor, a subtle confidence that seemed to radiate from within.

"Maestro, I think you may have found your inspiration," Marcus said softly, nodding towards Lisa.

Leonardo followed Marcus's gaze and smiled. "You may be right, my friend. Lisa, would you be willing to sit for a portrait?"

Lisa looked surprised but intrigued. "I would be honoured, Maestro."

Over the next few weeks, Marcus watched as Leonardo worked tirelessly on the painting. He captured every nuance of Lisa's expression, every subtle shift in her smile. Marcus often found himself in the workshop, offering encouragement and observing the creative process.

One day, as Leonardo was putting the finishing touches to the painting, he turned to Marcus with a thoughtful expression. "You know, Marcus, it was your suggestion that led me to this moment. Your keen eye and insight have been invaluable."

Marcus smiled, feeling a sense of pride and fulfillment. "I'm just glad I could help, Maestro. The world will be forever changed by your work."

As the final brushstroke was applied, Leonardo stepped back to admire the painting. The woman on the canvas seemed to come alive, her smile a perfect blend of warmth and mystery. It was a masterpiece, a testament to Leonardo's genius and the inspiration he had found in Lisa—and, in a small way, in Marcus.

The painting would go on to become one of the most famous works of art in history, known to the world as the Mona Lisa. And though Marcus's role in its creation would remain a secret, he knew that he had been a part of something truly extraordinary.

Chapter Eleven: The Witch Trials of Salem.

The year was 1692, and the small town of Salem, Massachusetts, was gripped by a wave of hysteria. The infamous Salem witch trials had begun, fueled by fear, superstition, and a fervent desire to root out perceived evil. Accusations of witchcraft spread like wildfire, and many innocent people found themselves facing the gallows.

Marcus, ever the wanderer, had arrived in Salem just as the trials were reaching their peak. He had seen many forms of injustice over the centuries, but the fervor and cruelty of the witch hunts were particularly abhorrent. The town was a cauldron of fear and suspicion, and the lives of many hung in the balance.

One evening, as Marcus walked through the town square, he overheard a group of townspeople discussing the latest trial. A woman named Sarah had been accused of witchcraft, her beauty and independence making her a target for those who sought to control and condemn. The charges against her were baseless, but in the climate of fear that gripped Salem, reason and justice had been cast aside.

Determined to help, Marcus made his way to the meetinghouse where the trials were being held. The room was filled with townspeople, their faces a mixture of fear and righteous indignation. At the front of the room, Sarah stood before the magistrates, her hands bound and her eyes defiant.

"Sarah Good," the magistrate intoned, "you stand accused of witchcraft, of beguiling men with your beauty and consorting with the devil. How do you plead?"

"I am innocent," Sarah replied, her voice steady despite the fear that gripped her heart. "I have done no wrong."

The crowd murmured, their suspicion and fear palpable. Marcus watched from the back of the room, his mind racing as he considered how best to intervene. He knew that a direct confrontation would only make matters worse, but he could not stand by and let an innocent woman be condemned.

As the trial continued, Marcus slipped out of the meetinghouse and made his way to the jail where Sarah was being held. The building was guarded, but Marcus's centuries of experience had taught him how to move unseen. He waited for the cover of darkness, then approached the jail with silent determination.

Using a set of lockpicks he had acquired over the years, Marcus quickly and quietly unlocked the door to Sarah's cell. She looked up in surprise as he entered, her eyes wide with a mixture of hope and fear.

"Who are you?" she whispered, her voice trembling.

"A friend," Marcus replied softly. "I'm here to help you. We need to leave now, before they realise you're gone."

Sarah hesitated for a moment, then nodded. "Thank you," she said, her voice filled with gratitude. "I don't know how to repay you."

"There's no need," Marcus said, helping her to her feet. "Let's go."

They moved quickly and quietly through the darkened streets of Salem, avoiding the patrols and slipping into the shadows whenever they heard footsteps. Marcus led Sarah to the edge of town, where he had prepared a hidden refuge in the woods.

As they reached the safety of the trees, Sarah turned to Marcus, her eyes filled with tears. "Why are you doing this?" she asked. "Why risk your life for me?"

Marcus looked into her eyes, his expression somber. "I've seen too much injustice in my life," he said. "I couldn't stand by and let them take you. You deserve a chance to live, to be free."

Sarah nodded, her gratitude evident. "Thank you," she said again. "I don't know what I would have done without you."

In the days that followed, Marcus and Sarah remained hidden in the woods, waiting for the hysteria in Salem to die down. Marcus used his knowledge of the land to provide for them, and they spent their time talking and getting to know each other. Sarah's strength and resilience impressed Marcus, and he found himself drawn to her in a way he had not felt in a long time.

As the weeks passed, the fervor in Salem began to subside, and the witch trials came to an end. Marcus knew that it was time for Sarah to start a new life, far from the fear and suspicion that had nearly destroyed her.

"I have friends in Boston," Marcus said one evening as they sat by the fire. "They can help you start over, give you a chance to build a new life."

Sarah looked at him, her eyes filled with gratitude and sadness. "What about you?" she asked. "Will you come with me?"

Marcus shook his head, his heart heavy. "I can't," he said softly. "My journey isn't over. There are still so many people who need help, so many wrongs to be righted."

Sarah nodded, understanding. "Thank you, Marcus," she said, her voice filled with emotion. "You've given me a second chance. I'll never forget you."

They embraced, and Marcus felt a pang of sorrow as he realised that he would once again be leaving someone he cared about. But he knew that his path was one of eternal wandering, driven by a commitment to helping those in need and seeking redemption for his past sins.

As Sarah made her way to Boston, Marcus continued his journey, he knew that the road ahead would be filled with challenges, his eternal wanderings continued, guided by a purpose that transcended time.

Chapter Twelve: The Wild Child of Songy.

In September 1731, Marcus found himself wandering through the picturesque countryside of Champagne, France. The rolling vineyards and quaint villages provided a stark contrast to the turmoil he had witnessed in other parts of the world. He had come to Songy, a small village known for its orchards and serene landscapes, seeking a brief respite from his eternal journey.

One afternoon, as he strolled near an orchard, Marcus noticed a commotion. Villagers were shouting and pointing towards a tree where a strange girl was perched among the branches. She was dark-skinned, barefoot, and clad in animal skins, clutching a club in her hand. Marcus watched as a dog from the village lunged at her, only to be struck down with a single, powerful blow. The girl then swiftly climbed higher into the tree, disappearing among the leaves.

Intrigued and concerned, Marcus approached the villagers. "Who is she?" he asked, his voice calm and steady.

"We don't know," one of the villagers replied, shaking his head. "She appeared out of nowhere, stealing apples from the orchard. She's wild, like an animal."

Marcus's curiosity was piqued. He had encountered many unusual individuals in his long life, but this girl was unlike any he had seen before. Determined to help, he approached the tree cautiously, speaking in soothing tones.

"Come down," he called gently. "I won't hurt you."

The girl responded with a series of shrieks and growls, her eyes wild with fear and defiance. Marcus persisted, his voice steady and reassuring.

After what felt like hours, the girl began to descend, her movements cautious and wary. When she finally reached the ground, Marcus moved swiftly, capturing her with a firm but gentle grip.

The villagers gathered around, their expressions a mix of curiosity and apprehension. Marcus estimated that the girl was between 10 and 18 years old, though her wild appearance made it difficult to be certain. He decided to take her to the village, where she could be properly cared for.

After a thorough washing, it was revealed that the girl was actually fair-skinned. Her long, claw-like nails were trimmed, and she was given clean clothes to wear. Despite these changes, her behavior remained feral. She spoke only in shrieks and growls, and she astonished the villagers by eating raw meat with a voracious appetite.

Marcus observed her closely, trying to understand her plight. He noticed that when she was forced to eat cooked meat, she couldn't keep it down. Her body seemed to reject the "civilized diet" the villagers provided, and her teeth began to fall out, unable to cope with the new food.

Days turned into weeks, and Marcus continued to care for the girl, whom the villagers had begun to call "La Sauvage." He tried to teach her basic words and gestures, but progress was slow. She remained distrustful and wary, her eyes always scanning for potential threats.

One evening, as Marcus sat by the fire, the girl approached him cautiously. She had begun to recognise him as a protector, someone who meant her no harm. She sat beside him, her eyes reflecting the flickering flames.

"Who are you?" Marcus asked softly, though he knew she couldn't answer.

The girl tilted her head, her expression unreadable. She reached out and touched his hand, a tentative gesture of trust. Marcus felt a pang of sorrow for the life she must have led, isolated and wild.

As the months passed, Marcus continued to care for La Sauvage, though he knew that fully integrating her into society might never be possible. She had lived too long in the wild, her instincts too deeply ingrained. Yet, he remained patient, offering her kindness and understanding.

In time, the villagers grew accustomed to her presence, and she became a part of their community, albeit on the fringes. Marcus knew that he would eventually have to move on, but he took solace in the knowledge that he had made a difference in her life, however small.

As he prepared to leave Songy, Marcus looked back at the village one last time. La Sauvage stood at the edge of the orchard, watching him with those same wild eyes. He raised a hand in farewell, and she responded with a small, hesitant wave.

Marcus turned and walked away, his heart heavy with the weight of another life touched by his eternal journey. He knew that the road ahead would bring new challenges and new souls in need of help. And so, he continued on, driven by the hope that, in some small way, he could bring light to a world often shrouded in darkness.

Chapter Thirteen: The Revolution's Shadow.

The year was 1793, and Paris was a city engulfed in chaos. The French Revolution had reached its bloody zenith, and the guillotine's blade fell with relentless regularity. Marcus, now centuries into his eternal wanderings, found himself in the heart of this turmoil. He had seen many revolutions, but the fervor and brutality of this one were unparalleled.

One evening, as the sun dipped below the horizon, casting long shadows over the cobblestone streets, Marcus moved through the throngs of people gathered at the Place de la Révolution. The air was thick with tension and the scent of fear. He had come to offer what help he could, to save lives in a time when life seemed so cheap.

As he approached the guillotine, his eyes were drawn to a young woman being led to her execution. Her beauty was striking, even in her disheveled state. Her eyes, filled with a mixture of defiance and despair, met his, and in that moment, Marcus felt a familiar pang of sorrow. He had seen too many innocent lives lost, and he could not stand by and watch another.

With a swift and calculated move, Marcus pushed through the crowd, his years of military training guiding his actions. He reached the platform just as the executioner was about to lower the blade. In a blur of motion, Marcus disarmed the guards and swept the woman into his arms. The crowd erupted in chaos, but Marcus's determination was unyielding.

"Hold on," he whispered to her as he fought his way through the panicked masses.

They fled through the narrow streets of Paris, the sounds of pursuit growing fainter with each turn. Marcus knew the city well, having walked its streets in different eras. He led her to a hidden passageway that opened into the catacombs beneath the city. There, in the damp and dark, they found a moment of respite.

"Who are you?" the woman asked, her voice trembling.

"My name is Marcus," he replied, his eyes softening as he looked at her. "And you?"

"Elisabeth," she said, her voice barely above a whisper. "Thank you for saving me."

"We're not safe yet," Marcus said, his tone urgent. "We need to get out of Paris."

Over the next few days, Marcus and Elisabeth made their way to the coast, avoiding patrols and relying on Marcus's knowledge of the land. They secured passage on a ship bound for England, and as they sailed across the Channel, a bond began to form between them.

In England, they found refuge in a quiet village. Marcus, ever the protector, ensured Elisabeth was safe and comfortable. As the days turned into weeks, their connection deepened. Marcus found himself drawn to her in a way he had not felt in centuries. Elisabeth, too, felt a growing affection for the man who had saved her life.

One evening, as they walked along the cliffs overlooking the sea, Marcus took Elisabeth's hand. "Elisabeth, I have something to tell you," he began, his voice heavy with the weight of his secret.

She looked at him, her eyes filled with trust and curiosity. "What is it, Marcus?"

"I am not like other men," he said, his gaze fixed on the horizon. "I am cursed to live forever. I have walked this earth for nearly two thousand years, seeking redemption for my past sins."

Elisabeth's eyes widened in shock, but she did not pull away. "You mean... you are immortal?"

"Yes," Marcus replied, his voice tinged with sorrow. "I have seen countless lives come and go, and I have loved and lost more times than I can bear. I wish to marry you, Elisabeth, but I know that it would only lead to more heartache. You would grow old, and I would remain the same. I cannot bear the thought of losing you."

Tears welled in Elisabeth's eyes as she realized the depth of his pain. "Marcus, I love you," she said, her voice breaking. "But I understand. I cannot ask you to endure that kind of suffering."

They stood in silence, the weight of their unspoken love hanging between them. Finally, Marcus spoke. "I will always be here for you, Elisabeth. I will protect you and ensure your happiness, even if it means I must keep my distance."

Elisabeth nodded, her heart heavy with the knowledge of what could never be. "Thank you, Marcus. For everything."

As they walked back to the village, hand in hand, they both knew that their love, though unfulfilled, would remain a cherished memory. Marcus continued his eternal journey, carrying with him the bittersweet reminder of a love that could never be, yet had touched his immortal heart in a way that time could never erase.

Chapter Fourteen: The Path to Freedom.

The year was 1863, and America was torn apart by the Civil War. The nation was divided, with the Union fighting to preserve the country and end the institution of slavery, while the Confederacy sought to maintain their way of life. Amidst the chaos and bloodshed, Marcus found himself once again drawn to a cause that resonated deeply with his quest for redemption.

He had traveled to the southern states, where the plight of African Slaves weighed heavily on his heart. The stories of their suffering and the brutal conditions they endured stirred something within him, compelling him to act. Marcus had seen countless injustices over the centuries, but the horrors of slavery were among the most egregious.

Using his centuries of experience and his ability to blend into any environment, Marcus became a conductor on the Underground Railroad—a secret network of routes and safe houses that helped Slaves escape to freedom in the North. He worked alongside abolitionists, risking his life to guide those seeking liberation through treacherous terrain and hostile territory.

One moonless night, Marcus found himself deep in the heart of the South, leading a small group of escaped slaves through the dense woods. The group consisted of men, women, and children, their faces etched with fear and determination. They had left everything behind, driven by the hope of a better life in the North.

"Stay close and keep quiet," Marcus whispered, his voice steady and reassuring. "We'll be safe once we reach the next safe house."

The group nodded, their eyes filled with trust and desperation. Marcus led them through the darkness, his senses heightened as he listened for any signs of danger. The journey was fraught with peril—slave catchers, patrols, and treacherous terrain—but Marcus's unwavering resolve and knowledge of the land guided them forward.

As they moved through the woods, Marcus's thoughts drifted to the countless lives he had touched over the centuries. He had seen so much suffering, but he had also witnessed incredible acts of bravery and compassion. In these moments, he found solace and a renewed sense of purpose.

After several hours of cautious travel, the group reached a small farmhouse hidden deep in the woods. The house belonged to a sympathetic farmer named Samuel, who had dedicated his life to helping escaped slaves find freedom. Samuel greeted them with a warm smile, his eyes filled with compassion.

"Welcome," Samuel said softly, ushering them inside. "You're safe here."

The group entered the farmhouse, their relief palpable. Marcus watched as Samuel and his wife, Mary, provided food and water, tending to their needs with kindness and care. The children, exhausted from the journey, quickly fell asleep on makeshift beds, while the adults shared their stories of hardship and hope.

As the night wore on, Marcus and Samuel sat by the fireplace, discussing the next steps in their mission. The journey to the North was far from over, and they knew that the road ahead would be dangerous.

"We'll need to move quickly," Samuel said, his voice low. "The patrols have been increasing, and the risk of capture is high."

Marcus nodded, his expression resolute. "We'll leave at first light. The sooner we reach the next safe house, the better."

Samuel placed a hand on Marcus's shoulder, his eyes filled with gratitude. "Thank you, Marcus. Your courage and dedication mean the world to these people."

Marcus managed a faint smile, his heart heavy with the weight of his past. "It's the least I can do. I've seen too much suffering in my life. If I can help even a few find freedom, it's worth the risk."

As dawn approached, Marcus and the group prepared to continue their journey. The air was crisp and cool, the first light of day casting a soft glow over the landscape. Marcus led the way, his senses alert as they moved through the woods.

The journey was arduous, but Marcus's unwavering determination and the support of the Underground Railroad network guided them forward. They traveled by night, seeking refuge in safe houses and relying on the kindness of strangers who shared their commitment to freedom.

After weeks of travel, the group finally reached the North, their faces filled with a mixture of exhaustion and elation. They had made it to freedom, their dreams of a better life now within reach. Marcus watched as they embraced their new reality, their joy and relief a testament to the power of hope and resilience.

As the group settled into their new lives, Marcus felt a sense of fulfillment. He had played a small part in their journey to freedom, and in doing so, he had found a measure of redemption. The weight of his past still lingered, but the knowledge that he had helped others find liberation lightened the burden.

In the years that followed, Marcus continued to work with the Underground Railroad, dedicating himself to the cause of freedom and justice. He knew that his journey was far from over, but he was driven by a sense of purpose that transcended time.

And so, Marcus's eternal wanderings continued, guided by a commitment to helping those in need and seeking redemption for his past sins.

Chapter Fifteen: The Birth in the Mountains.

In April 1889, the Austrian-Hungarian border was a rugged and treacherous landscape, still gripped by the lingering chill of winter. Marcus, now centuries into his eternal wanderings, had found a temporary role as a guide, leading travelers through the perilous mountain passes. His extensive knowledge of the terrain and his unyielding resolve made him a sought-after companion for those brave enough to venture into the remote regions.

One crisp morning, Marcus was approached by a doctor, a man of middle age with a determined look in his eyes. "I need to reach a remote house in the mountains," the doctor said, his voice urgent. "A woman there is about to give birth, and she needs my help."

Marcus nodded, sensing the gravity of the situation. "I can take you there," he replied. "But the journey will be dangerous. The weather is unpredictable, and the paths are treacherous."

"I understand," the doctor said, his resolve unwavering. "But I must go. Lives depend on it."

With that, they set off, the doctor following closely behind Marcus as they navigated the narrow, winding trails. The air was crisp and thin, the snow crunching beneath their boots. As they ascended higher into the mountains, the weather began to turn, dark clouds gathering ominously overhead.

Suddenly, a deafening roar filled the air. Marcus's instincts kicked in, and he turned to see an avalanche cascading down the slope towards them. "Run!" he shouted, grabbing the doctor's arm and pulling him to safety. They scrambled to a rocky outcrop, the avalanche thundering past them, missing them by mere inches.

The doctor, shaken but unharmed, looked at Marcus with gratitude. "Thank you," he said, his voice trembling. "You saved my life."

"We're not out of danger yet," Marcus replied, his eyes scanning the landscape. "We need to keep moving."

They pressed on, the journey becoming increasingly arduous as the snow deepened and the wind howled around them. Finally, after hours of relentless trekking, they reached the remote house, a small, isolated cabin nestled in the mountains.

The door swung open, and a man greeted them, his face etched with worry. "Thank God you're here," he said, ushering them inside. "My wife is in labor, and something's wrong."

Inside, the scene was tense. The woman lay on a makeshift bed, her face pale and contorted with pain. The doctor quickly assessed the situation, his expression grim. "The baby is breeched," he said. "I need to turn it, or both mother and child could die."

Marcus watched as the doctor worked with skill and precision, his hands steady despite the dire circumstances. The woman's cries filled the room, but the doctor remained focused, his determination unwavering. After what felt like an eternity, the doctor finally managed to turn the baby.

"Push!" he instructed, and moments later, the cries of a newborn filled the air. The doctor held up the baby boy, his face breaking into a relieved smile. "He's healthy," he said, handing the child to the exhausted but grateful mother.

Marcus felt a profound sense of satisfaction. He had helped the doctor save a life, and in doing so, had brought a new life into the world. The man, who introduced himself as Alois Hitler, and his wife, Klara, were overjoyed. They named their son Adolf.

As Marcus prepared to leave, Alois shook his hand firmly. "Thank you," he said, his voice filled with gratitude. "We couldn't have done this without you."

Marcus nodded, a sense of fulfillment washing over him. "I'm glad I could help," he replied. "Take care of your family."

Little did Marcus know that this child, born in a remote mountain cabin, would grow up to become one of history's most infamous figures. Fifty years hence, Marcus would find himself embroiled in a global conflict, the horrors of which would be unimaginable. The name Adolf Hitler would become synonymous with tyranny and destruction, a stark reminder of the unpredictable twists of fate.

As Marcus continued his eternal journey, he carried with him the memory of that day in the mountains. He had saved a life, only to see that life bring untold suffering to the world. It was a bitter irony, a reminder that even the best intentions could have unforeseen consequences. Yet, he remained steadfast in his quest for redemption, driven by the hope that, in some small way, he could continue to bring light to a world often shrouded in darkness.

Chapter Sixteen: The Battle of Redemption.

The year was 1900, and the Boer War raged across the rugged landscapes of South Africa. Marcus, ever the wanderer, had found himself in the midst of the conflict, serving as a medical orderly with the British forces. His centuries of experience had made him a skilled healer, and he had dedicated himself to saving lives amidst the chaos of war.

The sun beat down mercilessly on the arid plains, and the air was thick with the sounds of gunfire and the cries of the wounded. Marcus moved swiftly through the battlefield, his medical bag slung over his shoulder, tending to the injured with a calm efficiency born of countless lifetimes.

On this particular day, the British forces were engaged in a fierce skirmish with a group of Zulu warriors. The Zulus, renowned for their bravery and combat prowess, had launched a surprise attack, catching the British off guard. The battlefield was a scene of utter chaos, with soldiers fighting desperately to hold their ground.

As Marcus tended to a wounded soldier, he heard a cry for help. He turned to see a young British soldier, barely out of his teens, lying on the ground, clutching his leg in agony. The soldier's face was pale, and his eyes were wide with fear.

Marcus rushed to the soldier's side, quickly assessing the injury. The young man had been shot in the leg, and the wound was bleeding profusely. Marcus knew that he needed to act fast if he was to save the soldier's life.

"Hold on, lad," Marcus said, his voice steady and reassuring. "I'm going to get you out of here."

The soldier nodded weakly, his grip on Marcus's arm tightening. "Please, don't leave me," he whispered, his voice trembling.

"I won't," Marcus replied firmly. "I promise."

With a strength that belied his modest stature, Marcus lifted the soldier onto his shoulders, careful to avoid aggravating the wound. He began to make his way through the battlefield, his eyes scanning for a safe route amidst the chaos.

The Zulu warriors were relentless, their war cries echoing through the air as they pressed their attack. Marcus moved with determination, his focus solely on getting the wounded soldier to safety. Bullets whizzed past, and the ground shook with the force of explosions, but Marcus pressed on, his resolve unwavering.

As he neared the British lines, Marcus felt a sharp pain in his side. He glanced down to see blood seeping through his shirt, but he pushed the pain aside, knowing that the soldier's life depended on him. With a final burst of strength, he reached the relative safety of the British encampment.

"Medic! Over here!" Marcus called out, his voice strained with effort.

A group of medics rushed to his side, quickly taking the wounded soldier from his arms and laying him on a stretcher. Marcus collapsed to his knees, his breath coming in ragged gasps. The pain in his side was intense, but he forced himself to stay conscious, knowing that there was still work to be done.

One of the medics, a man named Thomas, knelt beside Marcus, his eyes filled with concern. "You're hurt," Thomas said, his voice urgent. "Let me take a look."

Marcus shook his head, his vision beginning to blur. "It's just a scratch," he said weakly. "Take care of the lad first."

Thomas nodded, his expression grim. "We'll take care of both of you. Just hold on."

As the medics worked to stabilise the wounded soldier, Marcus felt a sense of peace wash over him. He had saved a life, and in doing so, he had found a small measure of redemption. The pain in his side was a reminder of his mortality, but it was also a testament to his enduring commitment to helping others.

As the medics tended to his wound, Marcus's thoughts drifted to the countless lives he had touched over the centuries. He had seen so much suffering, so much pain, but he had also witnessed acts of incredible bravery and compassion. In those moments, he found solace and a renewed sense of purpose.

The young soldier, now stabilised and resting, looked up at Marcus with gratitude in his eyes. "Thank you," he said softly. "You saved my life."

Marcus managed a faint smile, his strength waning. "Just doing my duty," he replied. "Rest now. You'll be alright."

As the sun began to set over the battlefield, casting a golden glow over the rugged landscape, Marcus felt a sense of fulfillment. He had faced the darkness once more and emerged victorious, not through violence, but through compassion and selflessness.

In the quiet moments that followed, as the medics continued their work and the sounds of battle faded into the distance, Marcus closed his eyes and allowed himself to rest. He knew that his journey was far from over, but for now, he had found a measure of peace.

And so, Marcus continued his eternal wanderings, driven by a desire to make amends for his past forever seeking redemption in the lives he touched and the hearts he healed.

Chapter Seventeen: The Trenches of Valour.

The year was 1914, and the world was engulfed in the horrors of the First World War. Marcus, ever the wanderer, found himself once again drawn into the chaos of conflict. He had joined the ranks of the Allied forces, serving as a soldier in the trenches of France. The war was unlike any he had experienced before, a brutal and relentless struggle that tested the limits of human endurance.

The trenches were a grim and desolate place, filled with mud, rats, and the constant threat of enemy fire. The air was thick with the stench of death and decay, and the sounds of artillery and gunfire were a constant reminder of the peril that surrounded them. Yet, amidst the darkness, Marcus found a sense of purpose in protecting his comrades and fighting for a cause greater than himself.

One cold and rainy afternoon, Marcus's unit received word that a group of American soldiers had been pinned down by a German machine gun post. The Americans were trapped in no man's land, unable to advance or retreat without being cut down by the relentless hail of bullets. The situation was dire, and the need for action was urgent.

Marcus volunteered to lead a mission to neutralise the machine gun post. His centuries of experience had made him a skilled and fearless warrior, and he knew that the lives of the American soldiers depended on swift and decisive action.

As night fell, Marcus and a small group of soldiers made their way through the trenches, moving silently and cautiously. The rain had turned the ground into a quagmire, making their progress slow and treacherous. But Marcus's determination was unwavering, and he pressed on, his mind focused on the task at hand.

When they reached the edge of no man's land, Marcus signaled for his men to hold their position. He knew that a direct assault on the machine gun post would be suicidal, and he needed to find a way to approach the enemy without being detected.

"Stay here and cover me," Marcus whispered to his men. "I'll take care of the machine gun."

The soldiers nodded, their faces filled with a mixture of fear and admiration. They had seen Marcus in action before and knew that he was capable of extraordinary feats.

With a deep breath, Marcus crawled out of the trench and into no man's land. The darkness and rain provided some cover, but he knew that the slightest mistake could be fatal. He moved slowly and deliberately, his senses heightened as he approached the German position.

The machine gun post was a fortified emplacement, manned by a group of German soldiers who were vigilant and well-armed. Marcus knew that he needed to act quickly and decisively to take them by surprise.

As he neared the post, Marcus spotted a narrow gap in the sandbags that provided a clear line of sight to the machine gunner. He took a deep breath, steadied his aim, and fired a single shot, taking out the gunner with deadly precision.

The German soldiers reacted with alarm, but Marcus was already on the move. He charged the position, his rifle blazing as he took down one enemy after another. The element of surprise and his sheer ferocity gave him the upper hand, and within moments, he had neutralised the machine gun post.

With the immediate threat eliminated, Marcus signaled to the American soldiers, who quickly made their way to safety. The relief and gratitude in their eyes were palpable, and Marcus felt a sense of fulfillment that transcended the horrors of war.

"Thank you," one of the American soldiers said, his voice filled with emotion. "You saved our lives."

Marcus nodded, his expression resolute. "Just doing my duty. Let's get you back to the trenches."

As they made their way back, Marcus couldn't help but reflect on the countless battles he had fought over the centuries. Each conflict had left its mark on him, but it was moments like these—when he could make a difference and save lives—that gave him a sense of purpose.

When they reached the safety of the trenches, Marcus was greeted with cheers and applause from his comrades. The news of his daring assault had spread quickly, and he was hailed as a hero. But Marcus knew that the true heroes were the men who fought and died alongside him, their courage and sacrifice a testament to the resilience of the human spirit.

As the war raged on, Marcus continued to serve with unwavering dedication, his actions driven by a desire to protect and save as many lives as possible. The horrors of the trenches were a constant reminder of the darkness that humanity was capable of, but Marcus's resolve remained unshaken.

In the quiet moments between battles, Marcus would often think of the people he had loved and lost over the centuries. Their memories were a source of strength, a reminder that even in the face of unimaginable suffering, there was always hope and the possibility of redemption.

And so, Marcus's journey continued, an eternal wanderer bound by a curse but driven by a purpose, forever striving to bring light to a world often shrouded in darkness.

Chapter Eighteen: The Fall of Capone.

The year was 1924, and Chicago was a city caught in the grip of Prohibition. The streets were alive with the hum of jazz, the clinking of glasses in hidden speakeasies, and the shadowy dealings of organised crime. Marcus had found himself in the thick of it, working for the FBI to dismantle the bootleg operations that fueled the city's underworld. His primary target: Al Capone, the notorious gangster whose empire of illegal alcohol and violence seemed untouchable.

Marcus had spent months infiltrating the network of speakeasies and bootleggers, gathering intelligence and building a case against Capone. The gangster's operations were vast and well-protected, but Marcus was determined to bring him down. He had seen the devastation wrought by Capone's reign—the lives ruined, the families torn apart—and he knew that justice had to be served.

One evening, Marcus received a tip from an informant about a major shipment of bootleg alcohol set to arrive at a warehouse on the outskirts of the city. It was the break he had been waiting for. He quickly assembled a team of agents and planned a raid that would strike at the heart of Capone's operation.

As night fell, Marcus and his team moved into position, surrounding the warehouse. The air was thick with tension, the silence broken only by the distant sounds of the city. Marcus signaled to his men, and they moved in, their weapons at the ready.

The doors of the warehouse burst open, and the agents stormed inside. The scene was chaotic—crates of alcohol stacked high, men scrambling to escape, and the deafening roar of gunfire. Marcus moved with precision, his training and determination guiding him through the fray.

He spotted a group of Capone's men attempting to flee with a truckload of alcohol. Marcus sprinted towards them, his heart pounding in his chest. He fired a warning shot into the air, and the men froze, their hands raised in surrender.

"FBI! You're all under arrest!" Marcus shouted, his voice cutting through the chaos.

The agents quickly secured the warehouse, arresting the bootleggers and confiscating the illegal alcohol. It was a significant blow to Capone's operation, but Marcus knew that the real prize was still out there. He needed to find Capone himself.

The next few days were a blur of interrogations and investigations. The captured bootleggers were reluctant to talk, but Marcus's persistence paid off. He learned of a secret meeting between Capone and his top lieutenants, set to take place at a secluded mansion on the outskirts of the city.

Marcus and his team prepared for the raid with meticulous care. They knew that Capone would be heavily guarded, and the element of surprise was crucial. As they approached the mansion under the cover of darkness, Marcus felt a surge of determination. This was their chance to bring down the most powerful gangster in Chicago.

The agents moved silently, surrounding the mansion and cutting off any possible escape routes. Marcus signaled to his team, and they moved in, breaching the doors and flooding the mansion with the force of the law.

Inside, the scene was one of opulence and decadence. Capone and his men were caught off guard, their expressions shifting from shock to anger as the agents closed in. A fierce gunfight erupted, the air filled with the crack of gunfire and the shouts of men.

Marcus fought his way through the chaos, his eyes locked on Capone. The gangster was trying to escape through a side door, but

Marcus was faster. He tackled Capone to the ground, his handcuffs clicking into place around the gangster's wrists.

"Al Capone, you're under arrest," Marcus said, his voice steady despite the adrenaline coursing through his veins.

Capone glared at him, his eyes filled with a mixture of rage and disbelief. "You think this changes anything?" he spat. "There will always be someone to take my place."

"Maybe," Marcus replied, "but tonight, it's over for you."

The agents secured the mansion, arresting Capone's lieutenants and gathering evidence that would be crucial in the trial to come. As they led Capone away in handcuffs, Marcus felt a sense of accomplishment. They had struck a significant blow against organised crime, and the city of Chicago would be safer for it.

The trial of Al Capone was a media sensation, and Marcus's testimony was instrumental in securing a conviction. Capone was sentenced to prison, his empire of crime dismantled piece by piece. It was a victory for justice, a testament to the power of determination and the rule of law.

As Marcus stood on the steps of the courthouse, watching the city bustle around him, he knew that the fight against crime was far from over. But for now, he could take pride in the knowledge that he had made a difference, that he had helped bring down one of the most notorious criminals in history.

Chapter Nineteen: Liberation's Dawn.

The winter of 1945 was harsh, even by Russian standards. The biting cold seeped through every layer of clothing, chilling Marcus to the bone as he trudged through the snow-covered landscape. He was part of the Red Army, advancing westward through Poland, pushing back the remnants of the Nazi forces. The war was nearing its end, but the horrors it had wrought were far from over.

Marcus had heard rumours of the concentration camps, whispered among the soldiers in hushed tones. But nothing could have prepared him for the reality that awaited them. As they approached the gates of the camp, the air grew heavy with an indescribable sense of dread.

The camp was surrounded by barbed wire, its watchtowers looming ominously against the grey sky. The gates creaked open, and Marcus and his comrades entered, their rifles at the ready. The sight that greeted them was beyond anything they had imagined.

Emaciated figures in tattered clothing shuffled towards them, their eyes hollow and haunted. The stench of death and decay hung in the air, a testament to the atrocities that had been committed within these walls. Marcus's heart ached as he looked at the skeletal faces of the survivors, their bodies ravaged by starvation and disease.

"Comrades, we are here to help," Marcus called out, his voice trembling with emotion. "You are free now."

The words seemed to hang in the air, almost surreal in their simplicity. The survivors stared at the soldiers, their expressions a mix of disbelief and cautious hope. Slowly, as the realisation of their liberation began to sink in, tears streamed down their gaunt cheeks.

Marcus and his fellow soldiers moved through the camp, offering what little food and medical supplies they had. They found barracks filled with the sick and dying, their frail bodies barely clinging to life. The soldiers worked tirelessly, doing everything they could to provide comfort and care.

In one of the barracks, Marcus came across a young girl, no older than ten. Her eyes were wide with fear, and she clutched a ragged doll to her chest. Marcus knelt beside her, his heart breaking at the sight of her frailty.

"What's your name?" he asked gently.

"Anya," she whispered, her voice barely audible.

"Anya, you're safe now," Marcus said, reaching out to take her hand. "We're going to take care of you."

Anya looked up at him, her eyes filled with a mixture of fear and hope. She hesitated for a moment before allowing Marcus to lift her into his arms. He carried her outside, where the other soldiers were setting up makeshift medical stations.

As the day wore on, the soldiers continued their efforts to help the survivors. They found mass graves, evidence of the unimaginable cruelty that had taken place within the camp. The weight of the horrors they had witnessed pressed heavily on their hearts, but they knew they had to remain strong for the sake of those they had liberated.

That night, as the survivors huddled together for warmth, Marcus sat by the fire, his mind racing with thoughts of the day's events. He had seen the worst of humanity, but he had also witnessed the resilience and strength of the human spirit. The survivors had endured unimaginable suffering, yet they had not given up hope.

As dawn broke over the camp, casting a pale light over the snow-covered ground, Marcus felt a renewed sense of purpose. The war was not yet over, but they had taken a significant step towards ending the nightmare. They had given these people a chance at life, a chance to rebuild and heal.

Marcus knew that the road ahead would be long and difficult, but he was determined to see it through. He had been given the opportunity to make a difference, to stand against the darkness and fight for a better world. And he would not rest until that world was a reality.

Chapter Twenty: The Battle of Imjin River.

The year was 1951, and the Korean Peninsula was a battleground of clashing ideologies and relentless conflict. Marcus, now centuries into his eternal wanderings, found himself with the British army, part of the United Nations Command (UN) forces fighting to defend South Korea from the advancing Chinese People's Volunteer Army (PVA). The war had brought him to the lower Imjin River, a strategic location that had become the focal point of the Chinese Spring Offensive.

The night was cold and tense, the air filled with the distant sounds of artillery and the occasional crack of rifle fire. Marcus, now a seasoned soldier with countless battles behind him, moved through the trenches, offering words of encouragement to the weary men around him. He had seen the fear in their eyes, the uncertainty that came with facing an overwhelming enemy force.

As dawn broke, the PVA launched a massive assault on the UN positions. Waves of Chinese soldiers surged forward, their battle cries echoing across the river. The British troops, though outnumbered, held their ground with grim determination. Marcus fought alongside them, his movements precise and deadly, a testament to his centuries of combat experience.

Despite their valiant efforts, the British positions began to falter under the relentless onslaught. Marcus could see that they were being surrounded, cut off from reinforcements and supplies. He knew that if they didn't act quickly, the entire unit would be overrun.

"Fall back to the secondary positions!" Marcus shouted, his voice cutting through the chaos. "We need to regroup and hold the line!"

The soldiers obeyed, retreating in an orderly fashion under Marcus's command. As they moved, Marcus noticed a group of men trapped in a forward trench, surrounded by Chinese forces. Without hesitation, he sprinted towards them, his rifle blazing.

"Hold on!" he yelled, diving into the trench. "We're getting you out of here!"

The trapped soldiers looked at him with a mixture of relief and disbelief. Marcus quickly assessed the situation, formulating a plan. "We need to break through their lines," he said, his voice steady. "Stay close and follow my lead."

With a fierce determination, Marcus led the men out of the trench, cutting a path through the enemy forces. His movements were a blur of precision and power, each strike and shot executed with lethal efficiency. The British soldiers, inspired by his bravery, fought with renewed vigor, pushing their way back towards the main defensive line.

As they reached the relative safety of the secondary positions, Marcus turned to the men he had rescued. "Stay strong," he said, his eyes meeting theirs. "We can hold them off."

The battle raged on, the British troops fighting with everything they had. Marcus moved through the lines, offering support wherever it was needed. He patched up wounded soldiers, reinforced weak points in the defenses, and rallied the men with his unwavering presence.

Hours turned into days, and the fighting showed no signs of abating. The PVA continued their relentless assault, but the British troops, bolstered by Marcus's leadership, held their ground. The Imjin River became a symbol of their resilience, a testament to their courage in the face of overwhelming odds.

Finally, after days of brutal combat, the Chinese forces began to withdraw. The British soldiers, exhausted but victorious, watched as the enemy retreated across the river. The cost had been high, but they had held the line, preventing the breakthrough that could have led to the fall of Seoul.

As the sun set over the battlefield, Marcus stood among the men he had fought alongside. They looked at him with a mixture of respect and gratitude, recognizing the role he had played in their survival.

"Thank you, Marcus," one of the soldiers said, his voice filled with emotion. "We couldn't have done it without you."

Marcus nodded, a sense of fulfillment washing over him. "We did it together," he replied. "Remember that."

As the men began to tend to their wounds and mourn their fallen comrades, Marcus knew that his journey would soon take him elsewhere. The war was far from over, and there were still many battles to be fought. But for now, he took solace in the knowledge that he had made a difference, that he had helped to save lives in a time of great need.

With a heavy heart, Marcus prepared to move on, driven by the eternal quest for redemption and the hope that, in some small way, he could continue to bring light to a world often shrouded in darkness.

Chapter Twenty-one: The Winds of Change.

The year was 1963, and London was a city alive with the spirit of change. The air buzzed with the energy of a generation determined to reshape the world. Marcus, now centuries into his eternal wanderings, found himself drawn to the burgeoning counterculture movement. The "Ban the Bomb" campaign, with its passionate calls for nuclear disarmament, resonated deeply with him. He had seen the horrors of war and the devastation wrought by unchecked power, and he was determined to lend his voice to the cause.

One crisp autumn evening, Marcus attended a rally in Trafalgar Square. The crowd was a sea of banners and placards, their messages clear and urgent. As he moved through the throng, he felt a sense of camaraderie and purpose. These were people who believed in a better future, and Marcus was determined to stand with them.

As the speeches began, Marcus found himself standing next to a young man with a guitar slung over his shoulder. His tousled hair and intense eyes gave him an air of quiet determination. The man introduced himself as Bob Dylan, an American folk singer who had recently arrived in London.

"Hey, I'm Bob," he said, extending a hand.

"Marcus," he replied, shaking Bob's hand firmly. "It's good to meet you."

They struck up a conversation, sharing their thoughts on the movement and the state of the world. Marcus was struck by Bob's passion and insight, and Bob, in turn, was intrigued by Marcus's depth of knowledge and experience.

"You seem to know a lot about history," Bob remarked, his eyes narrowing with curiosity. "How come?"

Marcus smiled, a hint of sadness in his eyes. "I've lived through a lot of it," he said cryptically.

Over the next few weeks, Marcus and Bob became fast friends. They attended rallies together, debated politics and philosophy, and shared stories late into the night. Marcus found himself opening up to Bob in a way he hadn't with anyone in years. He spoke of his past, his curse, and the endless search for redemption. Bob listened intently, his mind whirring with ideas.

One evening, as they sat in a smoky café in Soho, Bob pulled out his guitar and began to strum a tune. The melody was haunting and beautiful, and Marcus felt a chill run down his spine.

"Marcus," Bob said, his voice thoughtful, "you've seen so much change, so much struggle. I want to write a song about that. About how the times are changing, and how we need to be ready for it."

Marcus nodded, his heart swelling with a mixture of pride and melancholy. "The world is always changing, Bob. Sometimes for the better, sometimes for the worse. But it's the people who stand up and fight for what's right that make the difference."

Bob's eyes lit up with inspiration. "That's it," he said, his fingers dancing over the strings. "That's the message."

Over the next few days, Bob worked tirelessly on the song, drawing on his conversations with Marcus and the fervor of the movement. Marcus watched as the lyrics took shape, each word a testament to the power of change and the resilience of the human spirit.

When Bob finally performed "The Times They Are A-Changin'" for the first time, Marcus was in the audience. The song's powerful message resonated deeply with everyone who heard it, capturing the essence of a generation on the brink of transformation. As the final chords rang out, the crowd erupted in applause, their cheers echoing through the night.

After the performance, Bob found Marcus in the crowd. "Thank you, Marcus," he said, his voice filled with gratitude. "You were my inspiration for this song."

Marcus smiled, a sense of fulfillment washing over him. "I'm glad I could help, Bob. Keep spreading the message. The world needs to hear it."

As the years passed, "The Times They Are A-Changin'" became an anthem for change, its timeless message inspiring countless people around the world. Marcus continued his eternal journey, carrying with him the memory of his time in London and the friendship that had sparked a song of hope and transformation.

Though he knew he would never find peace, moments like these gave him a sense of purpose. He had touched the lives of others, and in doing so, he had found a small measure of redemption. The winds of change continued to blow, and Marcus, the eternal wanderer, remained a steadfast witness to the ever-evolving story of humanity.

Chapter Twenty-two: The Return.

The year was 2024, and the world had changed in ways Marcus could scarcely have imagined. Technology had advanced at a dizzying pace, and the global landscape was a complex tapestry of cultures, conflicts, and innovations. Yet, through it all, Marcus remained a constant, an eternal wanderer bound by his ancient curse.

He had traveled to London, a city that had always fascinated him with its rich history and vibrant energy. On this particular day, he found himself in Hyde Park, a sprawling green oasis in the heart of the city. The park was alive with activity—families picnicking, joggers weaving through the paths, and tourists taking in the sights.

As Marcus strolled through the park, he noticed a small crowd gathered around a man standing on a makeshift platform. The man was preaching, his voice carrying a message of hope and redemption. Intrigued, Marcus moved closer, his curiosity piqued by the fervour and passion in the man's words.

As he approached, Marcus felt a strange sense of familiarity wash over him. The preacher's face, his voice, even his mannerisms—there was something hauntingly recognisable about him. Marcus's heart began to race as he pushed through the crowd, his eyes never leaving the man on the platform.

The preacher's eyes met Marcus's, and for a moment, time seemed to stand still. Marcus felt a jolt of recognition, a profound and overwhelming realisation that left him breathless. The man standing before him was none other than Jesus Christ, the very man he had helped crucify so many centuries ago.

"Brothers and sisters," Jesus continued, his voice filled with compassion and conviction, "we are all capable of change, of redemption. No matter our past, we can find forgiveness and a new path forward."

Marcus stood frozen, his mind reeling. How could this be? How could Jesus be here, in the flesh, preaching in Hyde Park in the year 2024? The questions swirled in his mind, but one thing was certain—this was no mere coincidence.

As the sermon came to an end, the crowd began to disperse, but Marcus remained rooted to the spot. Jesus stepped down from the platform and made his way toward Marcus, his eyes filled with a knowing kindness.

"Marcus," Jesus said softly, his voice carrying the weight of centuries, "it has been a long time."

Marcus fell to his knees, tears streaming down his face. "My Lord, how is this possible? How can you be here?"

Jesus reached out and placed a hand on Marcus's shoulder, lifting him to his feet. "I have always been here, Marcus. I have watched over you, seen your struggles, and felt your pain. Your journey has been long and arduous, but it is not without purpose."

Marcus's voice trembled as he spoke. "I have carried the weight of my actions for so long. I have sought redemption, but I fear it is beyond my reach."

Jesus's eyes were filled with compassion. "Redemption is never beyond reach, Marcus. You have spent centuries helping others, fighting against darkness, and seeking to make amends. Your actions have not gone unnoticed."

Marcus felt a glimmer of hope, a light piercing through the darkness that had shrouded his soul for so long. "What must I do, my Lord? How can I find forgiveness?"

Jesus smiled, a gentle and reassuring expression. "Forgiveness begins with acceptance, Marcus. Accept that you are worthy of it, that your efforts have meaning. Continue to live with purpose, to help those in need, and to spread love and compassion. In doing so, you will find the redemption you seek."

Marcus nodded, his heart swelling with a sense of peace he had not known in centuries. "Thank you, my Lord. I will do as you say."

Jesus embraced Marcus, a gesture of profound love and forgiveness. "Remember, Marcus, you are never alone. I am with you, always."

As Jesus turned to leave, Marcus felt a renewed sense of purpose. The weight of his past had not vanished, but it had been lightened by the promise of forgiveness and the knowledge that he was not alone in his journey.

In the days that followed, Marcus continued to wander the world, but with a newfound sense of hope and determination. He sought out those in need, offering his help and compassion wherever he could. The memory of his encounter with Jesus in Hyde Park remained a guiding light, a reminder that redemption was always within reach.

And so, Marcus's journey continued, an eternal wanderer bound by a curse but driven by a purpose that transcended time. He knew that the road ahead would be filled with challenges, but he was ready to face them, knowing that he was not alone and that forgiveness was always possible.

Don't miss out!

Visit the website below and you can sign up to receive emails whenever George Gentle publishes a new book. There's no charge and no obligation.

https://books2read.com/r/B-A-COLRB-JZZZE

BOOKS 2 READ

Connecting independent readers to independent writers.

Milton Keynes UK
Ingram Content Group UK Ltd.
UKHW030631071024
449371UK00001B/154

9 798224 879670